BIG BOY

by Tololwa M. Mollel

Illustrated by E. B. Lewis

Clarion Books/*New York*

4

Clarion Books • a Houghton Mifflin Company imprint • 215 Park Avenue South, New York, NY 10003 • Text copyright © 1995 by Tololwa M. Mollel • Illustrations copyright © 1995 by E. B. Lewis • Illustrations executed in watercolor on Arches 300 lb. cold-press watercolor paper. • Type was set in 16/20-point Garamond. • All rights reserved. • For information about permission to reproduce selections from this book, write to Permissions, Houghton Mifflin Company, 215 Park Avenue South, New York, NY 10003. • For information about this and other Houghton Mifflin trade and reference books and multimedia products, visit The Bookstore at Houghton Mifflin on the World Wide Web at (http://www.hmco.com/trade/). • Manufactured in China • **Library of Congress Cataloging-in-Publication Data** • Mollel, Tololwa M. (Tololwa Marti) • Big boy / by Tololwa Mollel ; illustrated by E. B. Lewis. • p.   cm. • Summary: Little Oli wants to be big enough to go bird hunting with his brother Mbachu but has to take a nap instead. • ISBN 0-395-67403-4   PA ISBN 0-395-84515-7   [1. Size—Fiction.   2. Growth—Fiction.   3. Africa—Fiction.]   1. Lewis, Earl B., Ill.   I I . Title.   PZ7.M7335Bi   1995   [E]—dc20   93-21776   CIP   AC

SCP   10 9 8 7 6 5 4

Oli didn't want to eat his *ugali*. He didn't want to take a nap. He wanted to go bird hunting in the woods with his big brother Mbachu. His mama said no.

"You are too little," she told him.

Oli protested and hung on to his brother but Mbachu shook him off and left for the woods, dangling his slingshot proudly around his neck.

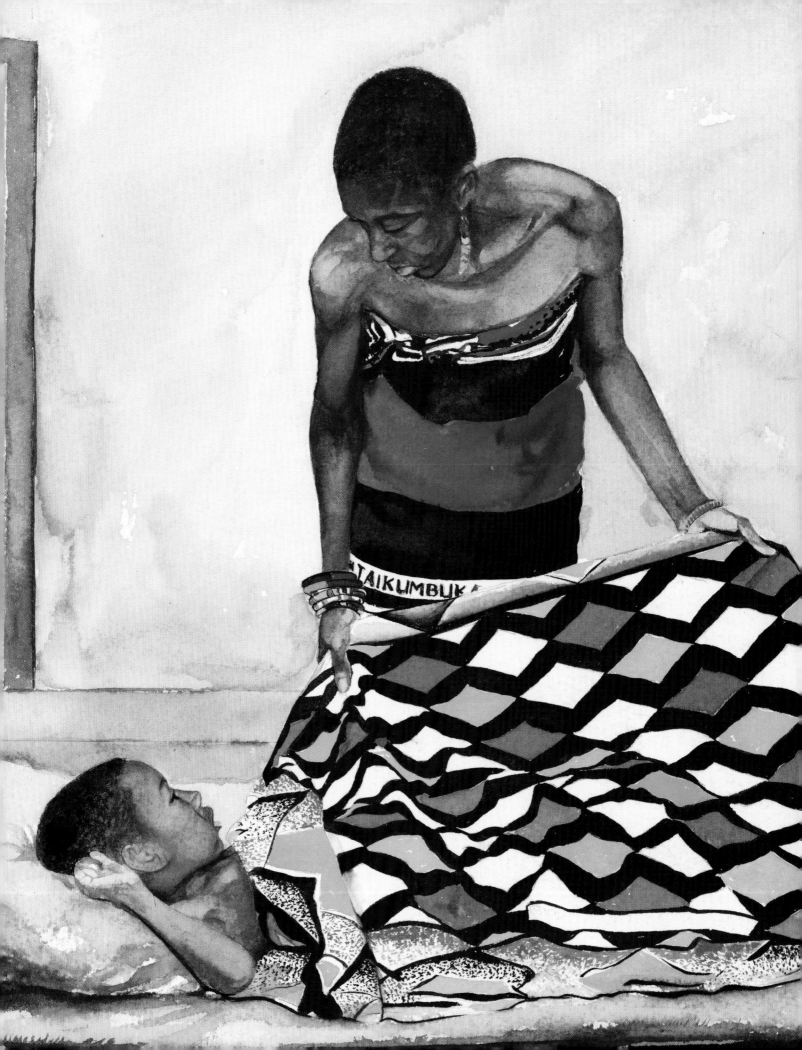

Mama spoke soothingly to Oli. "Here, finish your lunch and drink some water." After lunch, singing quietly, she carried him to bed.

"When will I be big, Mama?" Oli asked.

Mama smiled. "Only after many more naps, little one."

"I am tired of being a little one," grumbled Oli.

"But you are my only little one," Mama said, draping her colorful *kanga* over him. "Who else could I sing to and tell stories?"

Alone in the room, Oli stared at the smoke-darkened ceiling and wished he were big. Big enough to do without a nap. Big enough to walk side by side with his big brother in the woods. No, even bigger. Big enough to lead the way, Mbachu huffing and puffing to catch up.

Oli sat up and listened. All was quiet. From under the mattress, he pulled out his slingshot. Then he sneaked out of the house.

Soon he was in the shadowy depths of the woods. The air rang with bird talk and a million other sounds.

Suddenly Oli stopped.

A dozen feet away on a wild raspberry bush sat a magnificent bird. It had a long twitchy tail and striking silver wings. Oli raised his slingshot. But the bird hopped from one bush to another, and Oli followed. Finally the bird perched on a branch of a giant baobab tree.

Oli was so tired, he sat down at the foot of the tree to watch the bird . . .

. . . and then he had an idea. "I'll get closer for a good shot," he thought.

Soundlessly, he climbed up the tree. All at once, the bird turned and looked right at Oli. Oli gasped in surprise. It was Tunukia-zawadi! He recognized the magical bird from his mama's suppertime stories. Tunukia-zawadi bestowed upon wishers untold gifts and powers.

"Well," murmured Tunukia-zawadi, "what is *your* wish?"

"Oh, I want to be big. Big as a mountain and strong as the wind!" How Mbachu would envy him!

"Are you sure that's what you want?"

"Yes!"

"Have your wish," chirped Tunukia-zawadi.

And as Tunukia-zawadi flew away, there was a loud crack, and the branch Oli was sitting on broke under him.

Oli picked himself up and took one giant step. Immediately he was back in town—on a street by the market in front of his *baba*'s butcher shop! Mbachu gawked at him. Customers marveled.

His mama gasped. "Oli, look at you!"

"What happened?" cried Baba.

Oli proudly told them. Then he said, "I want to see the world. A drum shall be my companion."

With two ox hides and a huge water barrel he made a big, booming drum.

"Have some food before you go," suggested his mama.

But Oli couldn't wait to show the world how big he was. He pushed out his chest, beat his drum, and replied:

I'm *so* big I broke a giant baobab *tuntun!*
And one step took me home from the woods *tuntun!*
Food? *Tuntun* I need no food *tuntun!*

Off he marched to the beat of the drum. He strode from hill to hill toward a thick grove of *kuyu* trees, raising a cloud of dust.

Ch-ch-ch-cha-fyaaa! he sneezed. The next moment he stared in panic as a herd of elephants stampeded out of the grove. But they only brushed against his legs.

Oli hopped over the *kuyu* trees and continued his journey. He came to a dry village, where water sellers tried to sell him some water. "You are so close to the sun, you must be dying of thirst," they said.

Oli marched on, replying:

I'm *so* big I broke a giant baobab *tuntun!*
One step took me home from the woods *tuntun!*
And one sneeze set off a stampe-e-ede *tuntun!*
Water? *Tuntun* I need no water *tuntun!*

A path led Oli through a valley. He felt so happy and free he jumped for joy. When he landed, the earth shook. Boulders from a mountain came crashing down toward him. He jumped frantically out of the way, but one boulder bruised his toe.

As he examined the bruise, he noticed how tattered his shoes were. Looking up, he saw a city ahead.

"I'll go get myself new shoes," Oli decided. "New, tougher shoes!"

In the city, Oli found a shoemaker and asked for a pair of iron shoes.

"Iron shoes?" asked the shoemaker. "Leather shoes would be more comfortable."

Oli shook his head and replied:

I'm *so* big I broke a giant baobab *tuntun!*
One step took me home from the woods *tuntun!*
And one sneeze set off a stampe-e-ede *tuntun!*
And one jump started a mountain slide *tuntun!*
Leather? *Tuntun* I need no such shoes *tuntun!*

So all the city's shoemakers and blacksmiths worked day and night to make the iron shoes. At the dawn of the third day, they presented the shoes to Oli and wished him well.

As Oli marched on, the sun climbed into the sky and heated his iron shoes. At midday, he came to a poor fishing town. The sea was filled with boats, the fishermen selling fish on the beach.

To cool his feet, Oli jumped into the deep sea. A tidal wave rose high and almost drowned him. Then the wave swept ashore, drenching the fishermen and swamping their old, rickety boats.

Oli emerged from the sea, coughing and gasping for air. He felt bad at the sight of the soaked fishermen and their wrecked boats and asked what he could do to help.

"Bring us wood to build new, better boats," said the fishermen.

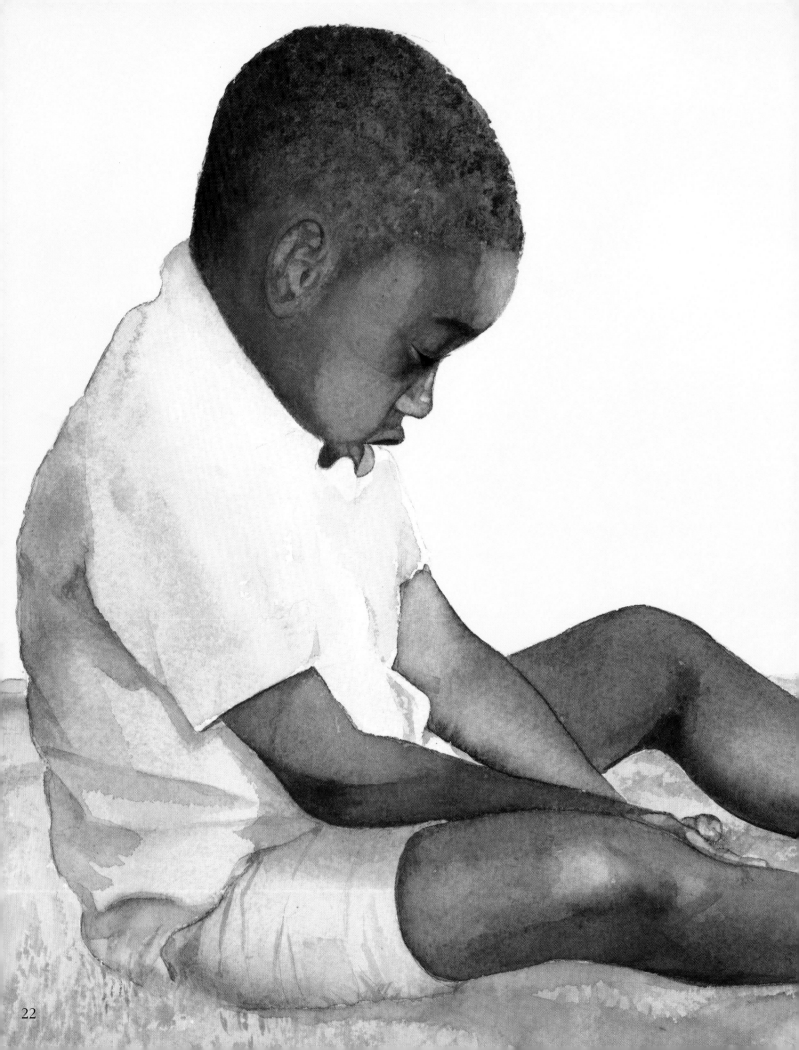

Oli set out to find wood. But his steps seemed shorter than before, his iron shoes heavier, and the drum less booming. His giant steps brought him to a canyon. He leaped across, barely reaching the other side.

His toe throbbed with pain. He stared at the savannah, stretching out hot and endless.

Now where could he find wood?

Oli thought of his close brush with the stampeding animals. He thought of the boulder bruising his toe. He thought of the hot iron shoes and the tidal wave that had nearly drowned him.

"I am so tired," he said, yawning, and sat down to rest. "I *wish* I didn't have to find the wood!"

A bird chirped overhead. Tunukia-zawadi's tail gave a funny little twitch. Down, down floated a feather. It touched Oli's face . . .

. . . and he awoke in his mama's arms at the foot of the baobab tree. She held him tight, trembling. "Oli, Oli, we looked all over for you."

Oli heard Mbachu calling, "Baba, Baba, here he is, here he is!"

And a moment later, there stood Baba. He looked annoyed, but Oli could tell he was also glad. Mama got to her feet. "Let's take him home," she said.

Baba nodded and said with relief, "Thank heaven he's safe and sound!"

Strapped to his mama's back, Oli watched his *baba* heading silently back to town. At Baba's side walked Mbachu, much too big to be on anyone's back!

Oli grinned.

How Mbachu must envy him!

He snuggled tighter to his mama.

It was good to be little, thought Oli.

Sometimes.

27

AUTHOR'S NOTE

This story was inspired by a motif I have encountered in African folklore, that of the prodigious child—a boy hero who is endowed with miraculous, formidable powers and is seemingly invincible. What drew me to this motif, which shows up in various African myths, epics, legends, and tales, is the point it makes about strength and vulnerability.

I have given the mythical element a realistic framework in *Big Boy,* drawing on contemporary life in my native country, Tanzania in East Africa. Consequently, the story has a few words in Kiswahili, Tanzania's national language.

baba (BAH bah): father, daddy

chafya (CHAH fyah): a sneeze; the sound of a sneeze

kanga (KANG gah): a woman's garment, a colorful and beautifully patterned piece of cloth. Sometimes the pattern includes a slogan—a proverb, saying, popular expression, or song lyric. Two are generally worn as a set. Traditionally, one piece is wrapped around the body from chest to shin or ankle. The other is worn over one or both shoulders like a shawl, or over the head.

kuyu (KOO yoo) trees: wild fig trees

Mbachu (mm bah CHOO)

Oli (oh LEE)

tuntun! (toon toon): the sound of a drum

Tunukia-zawadi (too noo KEY ah zah WAH dee): one who bestows gifts

ugali (oo GAH lee): a common staple food, stiff porridge made from corn, millet, or cassava flour. It is eaten with the fingers, rolled into balls and dipped in a sauce.